The Mysterious Cache

by
Candy Moore Myers

Dedicated to young readers

*I hope you enjoy reading this mystery
as much as I did in writing it!*

Illustrations by DeveoStudio.com

The Mysterious Cache

by

Candy Moore Myers

Table of Contents

The Mysterious Cache

1

Meet Heather

"M---O----M! M---O---M! MOM!" I yelled from my bedroom door.

I could hear my mother's footsteps pounding up the stairs.

"For goodness' sake, Heather! What in the world are you going on about?"

It didn't take my mother long to get the picture.

"Oh, my!" My mother sighed as she stood staring at the total mess in my room.

My closet door stood wide open. Some clothes barely hung from the hangers while some were scattered on the floor or flung across my bed. Not to mention my shoes! I

was going to have to be careful not to break my neck going into the room.

After my mother got over the shocking sight, she spun around like a top. She stormed back down the staircase, calling for Lizzie in the tone of voice that my brother Jeff, aka "Jeffie Techie," and I considered over the years to be the "voice of doom." In other words, we always hoped our mother wouldn't find us until she had calmed down. No question about it, Lizzie was up a creek without a paddle, as Jeff and I liked to describe it!

My little sister was not living up to her promise to our parents. She had just turned eight and had begged for a dog for her birthday. Since she was now in third grade, Mom and Dad felt that Lizzie was mature enough to be responsible for the care of a pet.

Of course, the only dog that Lizzie wanted was a dog like the Obama sisters had growing up in the White House. She had seen pictures of the girls playing with Bo in a history book at the Pandora Library. My parents, who were soft hearted, couldn't resist my sister's tearful brown eyes as she begged for a Portuguese Water Dog.

Now a ten-week-old Portie named Smudges (whose name, by the way, was spot on since the dog left smeared marks everywhere) resided in the Barkley household. I had to admit the pup's black curly fur with a white belly and matching paws were adorable. However, at the moment, I could literally skyrocket Smudges to Portugal, the country of its origin.

****

Three hours later, I finally had my room back in pristine shape. Removing the wet smudges was the worst part of clean up - YUCK! What a way to spend time on a Saturday!

****

Now it was time for my best friend, Pepper, to come over. After considerable pleading, I had convinced her that we *must* have special dresses for our first ever high school dance. If she had her way, jeans and a t-shirt would be ideal. Sometimes I wondered how we could be best friends with such polar opposite views on fashion. My philosophy is that a female should try to look her best when going out. She should be decked out from the top of her head to the shoes on her feet. The latest trends were the only option! Well, anyway, we were going to look through magazines and browse online for ideas of what to wear and how to accessorize. Since it was only a month before the big Pandora High School Homecoming weekend kicked off its festivities, we had to get on it.

The clock was ticking!

****

"Heather, I can't do this anymore!" Pepper said, flinging her magazine off the bed while sprawling out on it. "I'm going cross-eyed looking at the fashion models!"

Before I could use my persuasion skills to coax Pepper not to give up on our search for the perfect dresses, my mother was calling me from the bottom of the staircase.

2

Dog Walk

"This is bull! Why am I having to walk Smudges? Something is wrong with this picture. Just because Lizzie is grounded shouldn't mean I have to be responsible for her dog! I have a life!"

As I continued to rant and rave, all Pepper could do was giggle and giggle. It was a few moments later that I realized I had left Pepper behind bent over laughing hysterically. Of course, that made me stop and realize how crazy I must sound! I began to laugh with her. If anyone saw us, they might think that two laughing hyenas had morphed into humans. It wasn't until I felt a pull from Smudges' leash

that I was jolted back to my senses. Evidently, the dog had had enough of both of us.

"Come on, Pepper," I yelled. "I've got myself under control. Maybe I did overreact a bit."

"You think?" Pepper asked with a smile as we began walking to the dog park.

A few blocks later, with multiple stops by Smudges to smell and dig under bushes, we arrived at the dog park. As we neared the entrance, I bent down and unhooked Smudges' leash. Before I knew it, the puppy darted off to join other dogs running freely and barking their heads off.

"I can see that Lizzie has not trained Smudges to sit and enter the park calmly," I said with a sigh. "If I am on dog walking duty tomorrow, and I probably will be, I'll start training Smudges to sit and wait for a command before entering the park."

"She'll learn," Pepper said encouragingly. "Every time I come by here, I enjoy seeing all the dogs having a great time."

"Hey, look. That couple is getting up. Let's grab the bench before anyone else does," I said, darting toward the empty seat at a record speed for me.

Getting in a hurry was not my usual style. I believed that it was much more graceful to move slowly. Now Pepper was a different story. She knew only one speed – *fast*!

"Didn't know you could move like that," Pepper said, surprised. "Even those two kids were shocked that you beat them to the bench."

****

"Mayor Dalton and the town council made a wonderful decision when they voted to designate this area for a dog park in Pandora," I said.

"For sure," Pepper agreed. "It's definitely a godsend for people who live in apartments."

"Oops! I might have known Smudges would decide to do her business right in the middle of the park. It's pooper-scooper duty time!" I griped.

I could hear Pepper laughing as I began moving to do cleanup. I knew that she was relishing the situation I found myself to be in. It was a good thing that I had disposable plastic gloves in my pockets. My newly done manicure would stay intact.

"Well, that wasn't so bad, was it?" Pepper asked gleefully, as I plopped back down on the bench.

All I could muster up was a sneer, which Pepper responded back with a dimpled grin from ear to ear!

3

Imaginations Run Wild

"When we get back to my house, you've got to promise that you will look at dresses…."

Before I could finish my plea, Pepper interrupted by whispering loudly while shaking my arm and gesturing for me to look toward the far end of the dog park. "Heather, look over there! Something's up!"

Gazing to where Pepper was motioning, I saw two women having what I considered a vivacious conversation.

"Pepper, Pepper, Pepper! What has your indigo eyes gleaming? Don't tell me that your imagination is running wild again! What's so unusual seeing two well dressed women having

a lively discussion? You and I have them all the time."

"This is different, I'm telling you. These two women came into the park after we did. While I thought at the time that it was a little odd that I didn't see a dog, I figured they had children here with pets."

"Which is probably true," I agreed.

"That's just it," Pepper continued. "I haven't seen any kids come around them, let alone any dogs going near them."

"If that's the case, you may be onto something. Why would two women extremely well dressed, and by that, I mean decked out in designer clothes, come to a dog park?"

"Yeah, I hadn't even noticed that," Pepper interjected.

Her comment came as no surprise to me. Once again, I couldn't help comparing our two opposite viewpoints on appearances. While I believe looking your best is important, I would not be wearing high heels to a dog park. One should dress appropriately for the occasion.

"Look, they're leaving," Pepper said excitedly. "I'm going to follow them. Get Smudges and try to catch up with me."

Before I could respond, Pepper shot off like a streak of lightning!

****

"Come on, Smudges," I said, pulling on her leash. "Of all the times to be stubborn, this is not the time! We've got to try and catch up with Pepper!"

That's just great! Now I'm having a conversation with a dog. This whole day had not been going as planned. What was supposed to be a fun day combing through magazines and browsing the internet for homecoming attire had completely gone out the window! Saying this day was becoming a colossal disappointment was an understatement!

Before I could continue with the pity party going on in my mind, Pepper came rushing up to me, out of breath.

"Hey, you almost plowed me down," I said, somewhat annoyed.

Before I could continue, Pepper was waving a hundred-dollar bill under my nose.

"That reeks! Where in the world did you get that?"

"I – I –I, was," Pepper stammered while bending over trying to catch her breath, "following the women inconspicuously when one of them dropped it."

"Why didn't you try to get their attention?" I asked, puzzled.

"Ding! Ding! Ding! Earth to Heather! I was a significant distance behind them to avoid detection. I didn't know it was money until I got to it. Seeing what it was, I picked it up and was about to call out when I realized they were nowhere in sight. Looking around, I thought that there is no way two women could possibly vanish into thin air."

"That is puzzling! What should we do now?'

"Since we are close to the police station, I think we should turn it in," Pepper said. "After this summer with the Russian episode, I would like to believe I've finally gotten the drift about letting the adults take the lead. However, maybe we shouldn't say anything about following the ladies from the dog park. Since all our parents get together twice a month for Pinochle, Police Chief Hankins might mention something about it. I can hear my parents commenting about my overactive imagination!"

"Good point," I said, laughing. "Pepper, you must admit that you and drama have always gone hand in hand."

4

Bizarre!

"I hope I get to see Chad when we stop by the police department!" I said excitedly, picking up my walking pace.

Maybe my frustrating day was turning around.

Chadwick, aka an Icky triplet, and I had been going out since the end of our sophomore year. He was now doing an internship during the Fall semester of his junior year with the Pandora Police Department under the eagle eye of his father, Police Chief Hankins. According to him, it was no picnic with his dad in charge! Thankfully, he had been assigned to directly work with a new officer who had transferred from Galveston to ensure that there was no conflict of interest. While his brothers, Rick and Frederick, knew what professions they wanted to pursue in their futures - Rick, a professional baseball player and Frederick, something in the scientific field - Chad had not zeroed in on anything until after landing smack dab in both the 'Icicle' and 'Russian Espionage' nail-biting dramas. It was like a switch somewhere inside of him had flipped into overdrive.

The Icky triplets had always had more than their share of energy, which often landed them in hot water. Some people might even say *boiling* water! Their dad had even threatened them with military school. Anyway, the two nerve-racking incidents had gotten Chad obsessed with law enforcement. I could tell that deep down Chief Hankins was proud that one of his sons wanted to follow in his footsteps. When he didn't think anyone was paying attention, his face was one of pride when he looked at Chad. I found it quite touching. Chief Hankins gave off a persona

POLICE
Pandora (281) 555-1942
POLICE

as tough as nails with a no-nonsense attitude. My avid interest in studying fashion and cultural characteristics of people told me that Chad's dad was a softie deep down, sort of like a marshmallow.

****

We had barely gotten to the newly renovated, landscaped area outside of the police station when Chad came rushing out the door to meet us.

"I was hanging up posters when I saw you and Pepper through the window. You've just made my day!" Chad said with a ginormous grin.

"Right back at you!" I responded, giggling.

From my peripheral right side, I could see Pepper rolling her eyes. I thought it was sweet that my boyfriend was excited to see me.

As we entered the station, I could tell Chad was quickly shifting his focus back from his excitement in seeing me to his job. His whole demeanor changed to complete professionalism as he got back to work. Anyone not knowing that we were a couple and Pepper a great friend would think that two total strangers had come in off the street. Wow! Chad was going to have a great career in law enforcement one day.

"What brings you two young ladies into the Pandora Police Department today?"

Pepper and I raised our eyebrows as we looked at one another, silently signaling that we were impressed with him.

"Pepper found a hundred-dollar bill that someone dropped and wanted to turn it in to law enforcement."

As Chad took the bill from Pepper, I could tell by the way his nostrils flared that he could smell the rank odor of the money.

"Officer Rodriquez, can you come here for a minute?" Chad called out to his mentor. "There is something here that I think you might want to see!"

As the officer was coming over, Pepper and I gave each other looks of bewilderment. You would think seeing a hundred-dollar bill would be no big deal. However, Chad was studying the money as if it was an anomaly.

"What do you want to show me?" the officer asked casually as he joined us.

"Look!" Chad said eagerly, handing over the bill to his superior. "My friends found this on the street and brought it to the station."

Talk about an abrupt change in someone's demeanor! Not only did Officer Rodriquez's personality go from amicable to downright unfriendly, it was blatantly obvious that his displeasure was with Chad.

As most people would tell you, Chad is quite good at reading people. It only took a nanosecond for his radar to go off that the officer's ire was directed at him. His face turned bright red, completely covering his adorable freckles. I wasn't sure if he was embarrassed, afraid, or maybe a little of both. Once again, Pepper and I gave each other another look of confusion. Things were becoming more bizarre by the minute.

The tense moment was interrupted with loud yelps coming from outside. Talk about being saved by the bell. We were saved by the bark. Before entering the police station, I had tied Smudges leash to a stationary bench in front of the building. Evidently, the dog had been ignored long enough. This was one time that I appreciated a barking dog. I could tell Pepper felt the same. Mumbling our quick goodbyes, we departed.

5

Light Bulb Moment

Oh, my! I was struggling to untie Smudges. For some reason, I was all thumbs. To top it all off, Pepper was already a block away. What was up with that? It wasn't like we were being chased. Finally, I got the Portie free from the bench.

Just as I stood up, Pepper came sprinting up to me.

"Why did you take off like that?" I asked in an irritated tone of voice. "I could have used some help."

"Sorry. I was trying to run off some pent-up energy. You know that sometimes I have trouble being still. Also, it took every ounce of control I had to not start blasting questions at Chad and his superior. The daunting look on Officer Rodriquez's face was the context clue I needed to keep quiet. I am so thankful that we had decided not to say anything about the women in the dog park."

It was true that Pepper had more than her fair share of energy. She was a tomboy at heart. Again, when I stop and think about it, it is amazing that we are best friends with our thinking being like night and day. Go figure.

"Well, let's head back with Smudges. She needs to be fed," I said.

"Also don't forget, we're supposed to go to the football field and watch Miguel and your brother in a practice game."

"That's right! It slipped my mind with all the upheaval of the day!"

****

Pepper and I started walking back to my house in total silence. We were not known for being quiet. One of us always had something to say! In fact, my brother sometimes has the nerve to call me 'Gabby.' He says Pepper and I do more gabbing than anyone he knows. While Pepper just laughs it off, my blood boils. I have been known to throw a hairbrush or two at him when he riles me up. Whoever said having a big brother was the best thing ever hasn't met mine.

****

"Hurry up, Heather! The football game will be over before we get there!"

"Okay, okay, okay! Smudges has been fed and she is curled up sleeping in Lizzie's bedroom."

Pepper was anxious to get to the game to see her boyfriend, Miguel. They had gotten to know each other during the "Icicle" episode last spring. They made a cute couple, her with gorgeous red hair and sparkling sapphire eyes and him with creamy olive skin and velvety brown eyes.

"By the way, how is Lizzie?"

"Grounded for two weeks!"

"Oops!" Pepper responded. "I guess you were right that more dog chaperoning is in your future."

"Lucky me!" I said sarcastically. "Since Jeff is tied up with football practice, I'll be doing it solo!"

"I'll help when I can," Pepper offered quickly. "Who knows? We might even see those women again when we're out. Smudges will give us the perfect cover to do a little investigating."

"Hold on, Nancy Drew! Thought you were going to let the adults deal with any suspicious situations."

"That doesn't mean that we can't......OH! OH! OH! How could I have been so slow! I know what is going on!" Pepper exclaimed as she jumped around and around waving her hands up in the air.

All I could do was stand speechless with my mouth wide open until Pepper decided to share her latest revelation. I now knew what I looked like when I stomped around in my bedroom, waving my arms in a sporadic motion!

"Heather, how did we not catch on?"

"Catch on about what?"

"The hundred-dollar-bill! For weeks it has been on the news about a sudden splurge of counterfeit money in our country. My dad has mentioned it a few times at dinner."

"Hey, you're right! Mother recently told the family that she has been responsible for conducting new sessions on counterfeit currency detection measures and technologies to identify fake bills at the bank. Evidently, there has been an uptick on criminals passing off phony money. Mom says crooks have become quite clever in their endeavors of money forgery."

"Now that my light bulb moment has passed and we have an inkling of what might be going on with the hundred-dollar-bill, let's head to the game!" Pepper said as she headed out the front door.

6

Lively Banter Over Tasty Treats

The practice game had gone into overtime with our team winning. Now Pepper, Miguel, Jeff, and I were at Taborn's Ice Cream & Soda Delight Shop, celebrating the victory. Not that we ever needed any reason to indulge ourselves with delicious milkshakes, hot fudge sundaes, or banana splits – YUMMY!

While watching the game, Pepper and I decided that we wouldn't mention anything about the possible counterfeit money she found until we talked with Chad. We wanted to get his take on the situation - so it came as a complete surprise when my brother brought up the topic of fake money.

"Hey, have any of you been keeping up with the local news coverage of counterfeit money being circulated in Pandora?"

Pepper and I looked at each other like deer in headlights, which got the guys' attention.

"Heather, Miguel and I've seen that look between you and Pepper before. What are you two hiding?"

"Uh…uh," I began to stutter when Chad came racing into the shop. My boyfriend had excellent timing. Eyes were now off me and focused on him.

"Am I ever glad that my shift at the police station is over. After you two left this afternoon, I was lectured by Officer Rodriquez on professionalism. Evidently, I handled the situation of the hundred-dollar-bill you found and turned in all wrong. Instead of calling out across the room for him to come over, I should have documented the time the police department received the money, who had found it, the location it was found at, and if there were any other details noticed. All I managed to do, he said, was blow the situation out of proportion. The man went on and on and on…"

My brother finally interrupted Chad saying, "Hey, buddy, calm down before you stroke out!"

"Yeah, Chad," Miguel added. "I guess now we know why Pepper and Heather gave each other those weird looks."

"I figured you two would have shared with the guys about finding the hundred-dollar-bill," Chad said in surprise.

"We wanted to talk to you first before bringing the subject up," I explained.

"That's right," Pepper chimed in. "We thought the money might be counterfeit by Officer Rodriquez's reaction to the situation."

"That's what had me so excited," Chad explained. "I know Dad has been investigating every possible lead on the counterfeit operation going on in town. I thought the hundred-dollar-bill you found might help with the investigation. The terrible smell of the bill alone made me suspicious that it might not be legit."

"That seems to be a reasonable conclusion to me," Jeffie Techie interjected while the rest of us nodded in agreement.

"Obviously, I was wrong. Officer Rodriquez held the money up to the light and informed me it was not fake when I was able to get a word in to share my suspicion about the bill."

"Regardless of the money being legitimate, it still doesn't clarify why your mentor didn't stop us before we left and followed up with Heather and me on what he chastised you on not doing," Pepper said in her sleuthing mode. "Also, isn't it true that if anything is found and it gets turned into law enforcement, a receipt is given to the finder and after a certain amount of time passes with no claim made on the item that the person who found it receives it back to keep?"

Oh, goodness! When Pepper's inquisitive nature began to suspect that something shady was going on that meant the gang of seven (Pepper, Miguel, Jeff, Chad, Rick, Frederick, and me) might be drawn into another dramatic escapade.

"Remember, we told our parents that if we noticed anything suspicious we would share it with an adult," I reminded everyone.

"We did take the money to an adult. Look how that turned out," Pepper countered.

"You may be on to something," Chad said thoughtfully. "The more I think about it, the more I believe Officer Rodriquez's handling of the situation was odd. If nothing else, he should have commented on the putrid smell of the bill."

"Well, I for one think we should table this conversation for another time and just enjoy our ice cream treats!" I said, taking a big bite of my banana split before offering Chad a taste.

Everyone echoed "ditto" and began to savor every mouthful.

7

Counterfeit Research

Since everyone's curiosity (maybe not so much mine) had been piqued, the gang of seven were now sprawled out in my brother's room, researching counterfeiting. Chad had filled his brothers in on what had happened earlier in the day. Since the triplets' motto was much like the Three Musketeers' 'All for one and one for all,' there was no way that they were not going to be involved with what might very well be, in their opinion, an exciting undercover mission. Anyone who knew the triplets knew that they were adrenaline junkies.

All that could be heard for the next few minutes was clicking sounds as everyone (well not me – since I was determined that my whole Saturday was not a total loss, I was secretly viewing party attire for the upcoming dance) was totally engrossed in finding information on counterfeit operations.

I almost jumped out of my skin when Chad said, "Wow! I had no idea that the first time counterfeiting had been used as a tactic of war was during colonial times by the British when America was trying to achieve its independence."

Chad's statement set off the others sharing tidbits of what had caught their attention.

"Get this," Frederick said. "During the Holocaust, concentration camp prisoners were forced under the threat of execution to make fake British currency."

"Oh, my!" Pepper gasped. "A woman named Catherine Murphy was convicted by the English of high treason in 1789 for counterfeiting. She was hanged to death and later burned at the stake. Evidently this

brought about the Treason Act of 1790 to ensure the abolishment of burning anyone again at the stake."

"Gee," Rick added, "the only person that I ever knew about being burned at the stake was nineteen-year-old Joan of Arc!"

All of us in the room dittoed that she was the only one that they had heard about burning at the stake, too.

This latest tidbit of info had everyone a little shaken. I could tell that we were all thankful that burning someone at the stake had been banned a long, long, long time ago.

For the next few minutes there was total silence. No tapping on keyboards could be heard.

Finally, Miguel broke the ice by saying, "Before Pepper shared her finding, I stumbled on an article about how counterfeiting had been a part of the Civil War. A man named Samuel C. Upham was known as the King of Confederate Counterfeit. In fact, after the devastating Civil War, the Secret Service was founded in 1865 to combat counterfeiting."

"I found a cool story about an Austrian-American senior citizen, Emerich Juettner. He was known as Mister 880, and he evaded capture over ten years by the United States Secret Service for counterfeiting," Jeffie Techie shared.

"Wow! I just came across the same story. It's remarkable that he only was a counterfeiter of one-dollar bills," Pepper added.

"Yeah, he only counterfeited to survive during the Great Depression and after World War II," Frederick said, after locating the same story on his laptop. "Even though he was the worst counterfeiter, he was the most elusive one to catch."

By this time, everyone except for me was reading the same article. The others kept sharing facts about his life and how remarkable it was that he didn't get caught until he was 73 years old. To top it all off, everyone who heard his story couldn't help but like him and sympathize with his circumstances. The judge even gave him a light sentence of one year and one day which allowed for parole after four months, along with a fine of only one dollar. Due to international news coverage of Juettner's case, it led to a 1950 Academy Award-winning film, Mister 880. Emerich was able to live out the rest of his days in the suburbs of Long Island from the money he received from the film until he died at the age of seventy-nine.

I was barely paying attention to the conversation, when I realized that my brother was speaking to me.

"Hey, Sis, you haven't said one word during the discussion. What are you looking at over there?"

Trying to not look too clueless, I quickly responded, "Uh, just listening to the interesting facts being shared. However, I thought we were trying to find info about the techniques on spotting counterfeit bills."

"You're right!" everyone dittoed except for Pepper.

While I was silently congratulating myself by giving high fives in my head for my quick thinking, leave it to Pepper to see right through me. Thankfully, she only raised an eyebrow.

I'm certain that she knew what I was really doing. It was extremely rare that we could get anything past one another.

"I've found some facts that might indicate counterfeiting," Chad said a few seconds later. "According to this article, some letters in the text may be shaped or spaced differently than on the genuine note. Other bills might have a forged signature."

"In the story I'm reading, lines on the money may be more defined than they should be," Rick added.

"It seems to me that a person would have to be inspecting the bills closely to spot any discrepancies between the authentic money and the fake money. A magnifying glass would come in handy," Miguel said thoughtfully.

Everyone was nodding their heads in agreement. Even I was paying attention. I didn't think I would get away with looking at fashion a second time.

"The report that I'm reading states that the use of watermarks, security threads, UV ink, and other devices have helped keep US notes difficult to counterfeit," Frederick added.

My brother explained further, "These anti-counterfeiting techniques have drastically reduced the circulation of counterfeit currency. Also, it has helped that National Governments work together to target counterfeiters."

"I wish we could have another look at the hundred-dollar bill Heather and I turned in. Chad, do you think it's possible for you to take another look at the Benjamin Franklin?"

"I did see Officer Rodriquez place it inside his top right desk drawer. But I don't see the point of looking at it when he already checked to see if it was counterfeit."

"Besides," I joined in, "Chad doesn't want to jeopardize his relationship with his mentor any more than he already has concerning this situation."

"Heather's right!" Chad's brothers echoed at the same time.

"What I can do when I go in on Monday is casually ask if anyone has claimed the money. I don't see how that would raise a red flag."

Everyone agreed that was the best strategy before the seven of us decided to go to the movies.

8

Suspicions Arise

I was on dog walking duty again. Pepper said she would try and catch up with me once she finished the article she was working on for the school paper. The Journalism Club met Mondays and Thursdays after school. My friend was thinking about going into journalism and possibly becoming an investigative reporter. Much like Chad, the two mysteries we had been involved with had sparked her interest in solving crimes.

Arriving at the dog park, I began training a leashed Smudges to sit at the entrance. I was pleasantly surprised that after four tries, she was obeying my command to sit.

"Good girl! You deserve a treat."

Smudges began wagging her tail. She knew the word treat. Obviously, Lizzie had been giving them to her frequently.

Feeling proud of myself, I decided to take Smudges' leash off and give the command to sit and see what would happen. Hallelujah! She sat and didn't move.

"Here, Smudges, have another treat," I said, bending down to pet her as she gobbled up the goodie.

As I was about to instruct the puppy to enter and run, Pepper arrived, causing Smudges to take off into the park.

"Hey, you interrupted my dog training!"

"Sorry! I could see from a distance that you were having success with the sit command. Maybe next time, you can work on the command to enter."

"Oh, all right! At least there are plenty of seats to choose from today."

"Let's go sit down close to where the two ladies were standing on Saturday. Maybe there is a reason that they chose that spot."

"Really, Pepper? That seems like a stretch to me. Oh, well, while you are sleuthing, I'm going to watch Smudges and wait for Chad's text."

On Monday and Wednesday afternoons, Chad completed hours for his internship. He always had a massive amount of homework to do on those days since he didn't have time to finish it at school. We couldn't see each other or talk on the phone. The best we could do was send a few texts back and forth. It was always a bummer!

While I was keeping an eye on Smudges, Pepper was moving around the area we were at, along with looking off into the distance to where she had followed the two women.

Finally, Pepper plopped down in defeat, saying, "I guess you're right. I'm overthinking..."

Before she could finish speaking, we heard a muffled noise coming from somewhere. The problem was that we really couldn't tell where the sound was coming from. Pepper raised a finger to her lips, motioning that we stay quiet to see if we might hear something again. We were finally interrupted when Smudges came running over to us, dropping at my feet. I could tell the little puppy was exhausted.

Picking her up and placing her on my lap, I said, "We're going to have to wait a few more minutes before leaving to let Smudges rest. Carrying her is not in my job description."

Pepper began to giggle and giggle. It was so contagious that I began to do the same!

We only stopped when I received a text from Chad that he was now home and working on an English paper due tomorrow. He quickly filled me in on what his afternoon was like. Arriving at the police station a little earlier than usual, he found his mentor to still be at lunch. Since the other officers were in the conference room for a meeting, he decided to check to see if the money was still where Officer Rodriquez had put it on Saturday. Sure enough, it was. Quickly he took the hundred-dollar bill out and took pics of both sides of it. He barely made it to his desk to complete some filing that needed to be finished up from Saturday when his mentor and several officers arrived back from eating. What was surprising to him was Officer Rodriquez stopped at his desk to tell him that an elderly man and his wife had come in after Chad left on Saturday to ask if anyone had turned in a hundred-dollar bill. The couple had been taking a walk when they stopped at an ATM machine for some money and the bill accidently blew away. They tried chasing it but couldn't catch up to it. Giving up, the two decided that the odds of getting it back were slim but was worth checking to see if maybe someone had turned it in to the police. His mentor said that it was a shame he hadn't been there to witness the relief the man and woman felt getting the money back. Chad wrote that it had taken his acting skills to a new level. Instead of standing up and telling his mentor that he knew the story wasn't true, he smiled and said it was wonderful that the money had been claimed. It had been hard for

Chad to concentrate the rest of the afternoon. He hoped that tomorrow after school the gang of seven could get together to discuss this latest development.

The whole time I was reading Chad's text, Pepper had been leaning over to read it, too. Finishing at the same time, we turned and looked at each other in shock!

"Oh, my," I said.

"Just wait until everyone hears that I actually saw who dropped the hundred-dollar bill. Even if Chad hadn't checked Officer Rodriquez's desk, we would have known without question that he was being dishonest."

"Pepper, you were right when you thought something strange was going on."

"I just hope that the others aren't upset with us for not saying anything about what we really saw on Saturday."

I could only nod in agreement.

9

The Plot Thickens

Tuesday morning Chad sent a group text asking if the seven of us could meet at Taborn's after dinner for ice cream. He knew that my brother and Miguel had football practice until five-thirty. I had texted him last night that Pepper, under protest, had agreed to go to Gilly's Boutique to try on dresses for homecoming before going home. He and his brothers were on chore duty at their house until their family meal. Everyone agreed that barring any unforeseen circumstances, meeting at seven o'clock should work. Now that we all were juniors and seniors, our folks weren't as strict about school nights.

Chad was careful not to mention anything about what the group had discussed over the weekend. Pepper and I agreed not to say anything about the info that we had kept from them until Chad had shared what he had learned at the police station yesterday afternoon. We were both dreading what the guys would say once they knew that we had left out some facts that led up to finding the hundred-dollar-bill Saturday afternoon. I was worried that Chad might get mad at me.

****

"What were you two thinking?" Jeffie Techie asked incredulously, while the rest of the guys were shaking their heads in utter disbelief.

After Chad had filled everyone in on what had gone down Monday at the police station, Pepper and I somewhat sheepishly shared the info that we had kept from them.

"For once," Pepper said, "I was trying not to blow anything out of proportion with my

sometimes overactive imagination. The whole situation could have been totally innocent."

"That's right," I chimed in. "All of us, including me, are constantly teasing Pepper about overthinking everything. We did what we thought was best, along with taking the advice our parents have preached to us on a regular basis: 'let the adults handle the problems.'"

"I understand," Miguel said. "However, the predicament we're in now is that without other concrete evidence, we can't go to any adults because Chad might lose his internship for snooping in his mentor's desk."

"Oops. I hadn't thought about that," Chad added nervously.

"Let's look at the pics you took of the money," Frederick said.

"I don't think we should do that here," my brother cautioned. "While we've lowered our voices for our conversation, I believe we need to be in a more private setting in case people get curious to know what we're looking at."

"We also need a real hundred-dollar bill for comparison," Pepper added. "Even though we know for certain Officer Rodriquez hasn't been honest about the money, the bill we turned in could be legit. It is possible that he wanted to pocket the bill for himself."

"True," Rick agreed. "Does anyone have a hundred-dollar bill?"

"I do," Jeffie Techie responded. "Since there is a half-day teacher in-service on Thursday and all extracurricular activities will be cancelled, let's plan to meet after lunch to investigate this situation further."

"Good idea! Come over to our house," I said. "Mom and Dad will both be at work. There shouldn't be any interruptions since Lizzie is grounded. Mom is making her go to the bank and do her homework under her eagle eye. Hooray! No baby-sitting for Jeff and me. Although I will have to take Smudges for a walk."

"Good thing dogs can't talk and tattle," Rick added.

Everyone laughed.

Now that we had a plan, everyone said their good-byes and headed home to finish up homework.

10

Proof Positive

"Oh, my!" Pepper gasped. "I would never have noticed that there were no teeny spikes on the seal at the right on the front of the bill."

"Now that we know for sure that the hundred-dollar bill is counterfeit what should we do?" Jeff asked.

The six of us were gathered around my brother and his laptop, looking at the blown-up pics of the fake bill. Comparing it to the real thing left no doubt that the money was counterfeit.

"Regardless of this proof, we can't go to an adult without new evidence. Chad's internship is still at stake," Miguel reminded us again.

Everyone was lost in thought due to the gravity of the situation.

Suddenly, Pepper broke the silence saying, "I think we should go back to the beginning."

"You're right. We still have no idea why those two women were at the dog park on Saturday for no apparent reason," Chad agreed.

"And don't forget about the strange noise we heard at the park Monday after school," I added.

"What noise?" the guys asked in unison.

"Oh, yeah! Heather and I forgot to mention that we checked out the vicinity where the two women stood that afternoon at the dog park. Seeing nothing out of the ordinary, we sat on a bench nearby watching Smudges while waiting for Chad's text. Out of nowhere, there was a muffled rumble. Neither one of us could tell where the noise came from."

I could tell by the looks on the guys' faces the new info had them baffled.

After a few seconds of silence, Frederick suggested, "Maybe we should also check out the area where the two women seemed to magically disappear."

"Good idea, bro!" Chad said, giving him a pat on the back.

"We should split up. One group check out the dog park again while the other checks out the location the two women were spotted," Jeff suggested.

"Since Pepper is the one who followed the two women, I'll go with her and check out the area where they disappeared," Miguel proposed.

"I'll go with them," Frederick volunteered.

"Since Smudges needs a walk, the rest of us can go to the dog park and look around some more."

Just as I put Smudges' leash on, a clap of thunder boomed in the sky, followed by a downpour of rain.

"Mercy! Where did that come from?" Rick asked. "The weather report for today was clear and sunny."

"I've said it before, and I'll say it again: 'a meteorologist can be wrong a lot and keep his job'. I truly can't think of any other profession that an employee wouldn't get fired for being mistaken so much!" Chad said.

"I can! I can!" I replied excitedly. "Someone self-employed!"

"Ha! Ha!" Chad responded back with a grin.

All seven of us burst out laughing!

Once we settled down, Pepper said, "Well, it looks like our plans for the rest afternoon will need to be put on hold." She was clearly disappointed by this.

Everyone nodded in agreement.

"Let's go to the family room and play some board games," Jeff said.

"Sounds good!" the rest of us echoed.

To top it all off, my sweet boyfriend walked Smudges so I wouldn't have to get my hair wet.

11

TGIF

"Pass it, Jeff!" the crowd was yelling from the stands.

About the time my brother was close to being tackled, he threw the football to Miguel who was at the five-yard line. Catching the pass, Miguel swerved from a defensive player on the other team to make a touchdown and win the game!

The Pandora crowd went wild. I could hear lots of people commenting that Jeff and Miguel made quite the quarterback and wide receiver. Some were even speculating about who might take their places next year. Those who said that some Texans considered football to be more of a religion than a game were not kidding. While I didn't get it, the expression of 'different strokes for different folks' popped into my mind.

****

Earlier in the day the gang of seven had decided to go to a classmate's cookout after the game. We were going to support Rick who had a crush on a girl named Amelia Alvarez. Along with her being in his physics class, he had watched her play softball and couldn't get over her talent. Not only did he think she was pretty, their love for playing ball was a bonus. Amelia's parents were hosting the get-together.

Since Chad had told the rest of the gang that Rick was trying to get up the nerve to ask Amelia to the homecoming dance, he had taken quite a bit of ribbing from the guys. Pepper and I thought it was sweet and that the boys were acting like total morons.

As we were standing around eating burgers and hot dogs, I noticed that Rick had finally

approached Amelia. They were talking and laughing. When I saw her nodding her head, I nudged Pepper.

"What's up?" she asked.

"I think Amelia has just agreed to go to homecoming with Rick."

Looking over at them, Pepper replied, "I think you're right. They're beaming at each other!"

As I was getting ready for bed, I thought that Friday had ended on a high note. Our school had won the football game. Rick had a date for homecoming. Pepper had agreed to try on dresses again Saturday morning at Gilly's Boutique. Later in the day, the seven of us planned to carry out the scouting mission that rain had put a damper on as soon as Chad completed his intern hours. This weekend was shaping up to be fun and exciting.

12

Discovery

"Wow, Pepper! That's the one," I said.

We had been trying on dresses for a couple of hours when Pepper came out of the dressing room with the most beautiful outfit on. She couldn't have found a more perfect dress if a fashion designer had been hired to make one for her. The beautiful, turquoise cocktail dress was short sleeved with a mirror cut-out in the back.

"While I'm not much for a fancy dress, I do like this one. I'll take it. Now can we get out of here?"

Earlier I had selected a gold cocktail dress with sequins around the short sleeves and neckline. It was perfect for my skin tone.

"Of course," I said, laughing. "You must admit that shopping for your first school dance wasn't so bad after all."

In a typical response from Pepper, she rolled her eyes, which made me laugh even more.

****

Later in the day, the gang of seven had decided to meet at my house for a short briefing from Chad on any updates. Jeff and I would be taking Smudges with us to explore the areas we discussed since Lizzie was still grounded. She was with Mom and Dad at a church meeting. We would be able to talk freely.

"Nothing out of the ordinary happened today," Chad volunteered. "I had to do data entry into the department's main computer for Officer Rodriquez. I did notice that the one time I had to go back to his station to ask for clarification on one of the entries, the desk drawer was open where he had placed the hundred-dollar bill, and it was gone."

"Which still doesn't answer the question of whether he recognized that the money was counterfeit or he just wanted to pocket the cash," Miguel said in a frustrated tone.

"I say we go investigate and see if we come across any clues that might give us the answers we're looking for," Frederick suggested.

The rest of us nodded our heads in agreement.

****

"Watch as I give the command for an unleashed Smudges to sit," I said proudly to Chad, Rick, and my brother.

"Good girl! Here's your treat," I praised her as I leaned down and gave her a pat. "Now, run and play!"

Smudges darted off like a streak of lightning to join the other yapping dogs. "Sis, Lizzie will be happy that her dog is learning to be obedient."

"I must admit that I have been enjoying walking Smudges – except when she wants to stop, sniff, and dig at every bush she sees. It's also a bonus that she's an intelligent dog and responds well to training. With that said, let me show you where Pepper and I saw the two women standing and heard the strange noise."

****

Meanwhile Pepper, Miguel, and Fredrick were retracing the steps that Pepper took on following the two ladies and seeing one of them drop something.

"It was here that I picked up the hundred-dollar bill. Looking up, I started to call out when I noticed they were nowhere in sight. I ran to the edge of the building and looked all around. It was as if they had never existed."

"I figure they had to have turned left. There is no way that you wouldn't have seen them if they had gone in any other direction," Miguel said. "They would have had to cross a road to go straight or to the right which would have made them visible to you."

"I agree," Pepper responded.

"It's bizarre that they would have gone that way," Frederick added. "My brothers and I rode our bikes down this street when we were younger. It's a cul-de-sac with two concrete buildings on each side connected on the end by a stone wall tunnel. Since the machinery manufacturing sites closed, these buildings have been vacant for years. Just look – all windows and doors are boarded up. There are multiple cracks in the structures. Some can be described as fissures. The weeds have swamped the back wall."

"I remember the news reporting that designating the dog park for this area was the first phase of a major construction development. The town council has voted unanimously for these two buildings to be torn down and replaced by state-of-the-art residential housing for seniors in January," Pepper shared.

"Yeah, that's right. My parents commented over dinner one night that the idea for this project was that older people would enjoy watching dogs playing, along with lots of children and adults being around," Miguel added.

"Not to mention the fact that this neighborhood would be getting rid of two eyesores!" Frederick emphasized.

"For sure!" Pepper and Miguel agreed simultaneously.

"Even though I think we're wasting our time," Frederick said, "let's go down this dead-end street and check it out."

The three had gone only a few steps when they saw a gap in the concrete wall. It was wide enough for them to slide sideways down the building. They shuffled about six feet when they came to a window well that had no glass with a ladder tucked inside to climb down into a basement.

"Well, well, well! What do we have here?" Miguel whispered.

He was in the front with Pepper in the middle and Frederick bringing up the rear.

"I'm not sure," Pepper responded quietly. "But I think we know now how the women were able to disappear."

"What should we do?' Frederick asked softly.

"Since it's broad daylight, I think we need to get out of here before someone sees us and go tell the others what we have stumbled upon," Miguel answered, once again in a whisper. "People could even be inside right now."

The three slid quickly out of the tiny space and hurried away from the building before talking.

"Hopefully, the seven of us can come up with a strategy that will give us some answers while not getting ourselves into trouble. I don't think I want to be grounded again. Something tells me it wouldn't be for just two weeks like last time. It might be until I go off to college which is almost two years away. UGH!" Pepper said with a grimace.

"Not to mention getting preached at 24/7!" Frederick exclaimed.

They all nodded and burst out laughing!

****

"Here's where Pepper and I were sitting when we heard the odd noise."

I plopped down on the bench while the guys walked and looked around. Nothing out of the ordinary seemed to stick out to them.

Just as my brother said, "This seems like a waste of time," a muffled noise like the one that got Pepper's and my attention was heard by the four of us.

"Wow!" Chad said excitedly. "That's coming from beneath us!"

"I understand why the other day you and Pepper couldn't tell where the sound was coming from," Jeff said. "If we hadn't been tuned into trying to hear something unusual, I don't think I would have known where the noise was coming from either."

"You're right," Rick added. "With dogs yapping and people talking to one another, a person would naturally assume it was a noise coming from far away."

"I'll go get Smudges and carry her while we go find the others and share our news," my brother said. "I think we may be onto something."

13

Surprises Keep Coming

As we were leaving the dog park, Pepper, Miguel, and Frederick appeared.

"You won't believe it!" the triplets said simultaneously.

It was uncanny how the three brothers often said the same thing at the same time. They were on the same wavelength 99% of the time.

When they finished speaking, the seven of us started talking all at once. Pepper and I were even flinging our hands around.

DOG PARK

Suddenly, my brother interrupted the chaotic scene by raising his voice like he often did on the football field. "Hold it! All I can hear is a bunch of gibberish! We're not toddlers! One at a time!"

Getting our attention, we looked at each other and began to laugh hysterically with tears running down some of our faces.

"Mercy! I needed that," Pepper said. "This situation has had my nerves on edge. You four go first."

Each side gave an account of what had been discovered. Eyebrows were raised with a few gasps heard. When everyone had finished talking, there was total silence. We all knew that Pepper, Miguel, and Frederick could easily have been caught snooping around. There was no doubt about it. At least one person was down in the basement by the sound that Chad, Rick, Jeff, and I had heard.

The looks on our faces reflected that none of us knew what our next steps should be.

Chad broke the silence suggesting, "Why don't we go home, get ready for a night out, and meet at Pandora Pizzeria around six-thirty. I haven't eaten since this morning and I'm starving. I think better when I'm not hungry."

Everyone nodded their agreement. Even Smudges barked a couple of times. She knew it was mealtime, too.

****

"I've been thinking about what our next move should be," Chad said after devouring two deep-dish slices of double cheese and pepperoni pizza.

"Whatever your plan is," Miguel interjected, "remember all of us are walking a tightrope in regard to our futures."

"Yeah," Pepper added. "We all have a lot to lose. Not counting your internship, none of us want to have restrictions on our freedom."

"Amen to that!" I joined in. "I do not intend to miss my first homecoming dance!"

"That's why I think that somehow, I need to get down into that basement and check out what is happening without getting caught."

"How in the world do you think you're going to pull that off?" Jeff asked.

"Before coming here, my brothers and I discussed inspecting the basement. Since we still have our walkie-talkies that we've used over the years for several of our well-known shenanigans," Chad said with a grin, "we will be able to give alerts on any sign of trouble."

"What if someone is in the basement when you get there?" Jeff questioned with some skepticism.

"That's a risk I'm willing to take."

Coming to Chad's defense, Rick stated, "He should be fairly safe since the noise we heard in the dog park is probably a great distance from the entrance into the basement."

"There should be several places for him to hide if he realizes people are down there," Frederick added.

"I don't know," I said. "It seems too dangerous to me."

"What choice do I have?" Chad asked. "Before going to my dad, I need to have facts that something illegal is going on around the dog park."

"You also need to determine if your mentor is somehow linked to the counterfeit operation or is merely dishonest by taking the hundred-dollar-bill," Miguel said.

"True," Chad agreed. "It is an extremely serious matter to accuse any police official of wrongdoing."

"If we can get to the bottom of what is happening," Pepper interjected, "we're also going to have to come up with a plausible explanation of how we stumbled on this information without causing our parents to go ballistic."

"You've got that right!" Jeff said.

"I say we make a pact that from this moment on, the seven of us will decide together about when and how we share the info, along with who we tell," Chad said in the most serious tone of voice I'd ever heard him use.

We all placed our right hands, one on top of another, in the middle of the table and nodded our heads.

****

After we made the pact, we agreed to get our minds off the dilemma and have some fun. I believed teenagers had a special way of compartmentalizing issues that allowed us to take time to chill.

Since it was now eight o'clock, we decided to go bowling.

About to get up from the circular booth that we were sitting in at the back of the pizzeria, Pepper kicked me under the table.

"Ouch! Why did you kick me?"

The guys, who were already up, sat back down, realizing something must be wrong.

Pepper said in a loud whisper, "Look up at the front door."

"Oh-h-h-h!" I gasped in surprise.

The guys looked, too. The triplets recognized Officer Rodriquez coming in with his wife and another couple. They had met them at a cookout for the Pandora Police

Department. Of course, Miguel and my brother had no idea who the four people were.

"Act naturally," Chad warned. "We don't want my mentor to suspect anything is up."

Miguel and Jeff quickly realized why everyone was looking toward the front.

Pepper and I gave each other knowing looks. Little did the others know that we were about to drop a humongous bombshell on them.

"If you don't mind, I need to sit here for a few more minutes to finish my Coke," Pepper said.

I knew she was stalling for time. Pepper was waiting for the two couples to be seated before we spilled the news.

While I could tell the guys thought Pepper was acting strangely, they agreed to wait.

A few seconds went by when Pepper finally spoke softly, "When we leave, Chad, you need to stop by your mentor's table and say hello. The rest of us need to stay a little behind and smile pleasantly. While we are doing that, I want everyone to take a good look at the two women."

I said, "Chad, you are about to get your answer to whether Officer Rodriquez is involved in the counterfeit operation in Pandora."

All eyes were on me. Pepper was signaling me to share the news.

"Those women are the ones that Pepper followed from the dog park. One of them dropped the money!"

Some say silence is golden. In this case everyone sat in stunned silence! The atmosphere was downright ominous.

14

Bowling Can Wait

Everything went smoothly leaving the pizzeria. Pleasantries had been exchanged at Officer Rodriquez's table.

As soon as we were away from the restaurant, Chad said, "I'm not waiting to check things out. I'm going into that building tonight."

"What about your walkie-talkie plan?" I asked.

"No time to waste! Since all our parents are playing pinochle at our house tonight, I'm sure that if my brothers and I go home, we'll raise their suspicions that we're up to something," Chad said.

"Which we are!" Rick and Frederick said at the same time.

Even though this situation was serious, the seven of us couldn't help laughing.

"Since this detective work could be dangerous, I understand if any of you don't want to go along," Chad said.

"Good thing that we're all wearing dark clothing. I'm in!" Pepper said.

The rest of us nodded our agreement, too.

****

Rick volunteered to stay at the top of the ladder to watch for anyone coming. We were hoping that since it was a Saturday night people were busy with some type of entertainment. More police officers would be patrolling the town on a weekend night. We did, however, need to be careful that we wouldn't be seen by the people watching their dogs run and play at the dog park.

One by one, we quietly climbed down the ladder with our phone lights on. Chad was in the lead with my brother in the back. He insisted that I stay in front of him. He had said that our parents would hold him responsible if I got hurt. While I sometimes felt Jeffie Techie could be downright annoying, it was at times like this that I was thankful he was my brother and willing to protect me.

"It is so cold," I whispered, shivering.

I could tell the others felt the same way since they were hugging themselves with their lit-up phones that shined lights in different directions and heights.

"It also smells awful! I believe the only people who would want to come into a pit like this would be for illegal purposes!" Jeff uttered with a cough.

"At least we now know why the money had such a foul smell," Pepper added.

It was eerily quiet except for the scratching noises. There had to be rats clawing around as we moved further into the basement full of cobwebs toward the direction of the dog park. No way would I remain calm or stay quiet if one of those rodents came near me.

I could almost hurl thinking about it. We needed to hurry this operation up and get out of here. The others must have felt the same since everyone began walking faster. We had left the first room and were halfway through the second when we could hear dogs barking. I think all seven of us gave a little jump of surprise, along with coming to an abrupt halt, causing us to stumble into each other. It was at that moment we realized that we were surrounded by counterfeit equipment and supplies that we had read about while researching the subject.

"I think I know now why the two women were at the dog park last Saturday," Pepper whispered. "If they could hear yapping from the dog park, they wanted to know if any noise could be heard over there when they were up to no good down here."

"That makes sense," I said. "But I don't understand from that distance how we could actually hear the jarring sound."

Freddy Boy, as we often called our science nerd Frederick, explained, "If you look at the numerous fissures in these old buildings, it is easy to understand that it is possible for sounds to be heard both inside and outside."

"Yeah, but what about the underground noise?" Miguel asked in a puzzled voice.

"In science class I've learned that sound cannot travel through a vacuum. There must be atoms and molecules present for vibrations to occur," Frederick said. "Actually, sound waves travel faster through the ground than they do the air."

"Listen, Bro, I don't think we have time for a science lesson," Chad interrupted. "We need to check this area over and get out of here quickly."

"Make sure not to touch anything. We don't want to leave any fingerprints," Jeff warned.

"I'd say the grating sound that can be heard over at the dog park occasionally is from moving some of the equipment around," Miguel said. "This area, being a confined space, would most likely cause some loud vibrations if these tables hit the walls."

"I'm sure the criminals would have preferred using the first room since it's more spacious," Chad said, "but didn't want to be visible from the window well."

While we were voicing opinions, I noticed that Pepper was unusually quiet. That was a signal to me that her overactive brain was devising a plan. I'd bet money that I wasn't going to like it, and was I ever right.

"Hey, I have an idea," Pepper said. "Heather, do you still have plastic gloves in your pocket that you use when you walk Smudges?"

"Yes. Why?" I asked cautiously.

"Take them out and put them on. Pick a couple of these one-hundred-dollar bills off the table and stuff them into my back pocket," Pepper directed.

Knowing there was no use arguing with her, I followed her instructions.

"Now let's get out of here and I'll explain my idea."

15

Plan of Action

Sunday at church, I was thanking the Lord that none of us got caught last night checking out the condemned building. I was sure my friends were also beyond grateful.

After leaving the dog park area, Pepper detailed her plan of how the triplets' dad could find about the hundred-dollar-bill that she found and turned into the police department without jeopardizing Chad's internship.

This afternoon around one-thirty we were going to put our plan into action.

****

"Thanks for coming with me to walk Smudges, Chad. It's more fun when I have someone with me."

"I invited my brothers, but they wanted to go to Taborn's for some ice cream."

We had only gone a block when Smudges yanked me toward the only bush on the block. She began sniffing around and pawing at something under the shrub. Stooping down, I removed a slobbery bill from her mouth.

"Gross, Smudges!"

As Chad bent down to see what I was going on about, he said, "Look! There's a hundred-dollar-bill."

"Same here!"

"Let's go show my dad. I don't think he would expect us to go the police station since we're so close to my house."

"Sounds good to me," I said with a smile.

****

"Dad! Dad!" Chad called out as he ran up the steps to his house.

"What's going on?" Mrs. Hankins asked as she came into the front foyer.

"Where's Dad? I want to show him something."

"He's in his study."

By this time, Smudges and I were up on the porch. As soon as Mrs. Hankins saw us through the glass storm door, she invited us in.

Before Chad could go to his dad's study, Police Chief Hankins came out to see what all the commotion was about.

"What's got you so excited, Son?"

"Heather and I were walking Smudges when the dog started sniffing and digging under a bush. Look what she discovered."

Chad's dad took a few minutes to study the bills before bending down and patting the Portie on the head.

"Way to go, Smudges! What a find!"

"Since we were only a block from home, I thought I should bring it here to you and not take it to the police station like Pepper and Heather did the other day. Pepper found a hundred-dollar bill on a sidewalk after leaving the dog park."

"I didn't hear anything about money being turned into the police department. When was that, Heather?"

"It was a week ago on Saturday afternoon. Since my sister has been grounded for two weeks, I have been on dog walking duty. Pepper and I took Smudges to the dog park."

Over the next few minutes, Chad explained everything that had transpired after we turned in the money. He even embarrassingly told his dad about Officer Rodriquez chastising him for not following the proper procedure when the money was brought in. He went on to say that he now knew what to do if anything was turned into the police station.

When Chad finished speaking, I added the part about how uncomfortable Pepper and I felt when Officer Rodriquez berated Chad and how we'd left during the conversation.

"Chad, do you know what happened to the hundred-dollar-bill that the girls turned in?"

Chad filled his dad in on what his mentor had shared with him about the couple and the ATM story.

"Tomorrow morning when I go into the station, I will check the records to see who claimed the money."

"What about these two bills that Smudges found?" I asked.

"Don't worry! I'll take care of everything. You two go ahead and finish your walk with Smudges. Chad, I would appreciate it if you didn't say anything about finding this money when you come in tomorrow afternoon."

"Whatever you say!"

We said our goodbyes and left.

16

Caught in a Trap

"Worked like a charm!" Chad exclaimed excitedly as he and I sat down with the rest of the gang at Taborn's.

Last night we had agreed to rendezvous for ice cream mid-afternoon. I could tell the others had been waiting a while. There were empty bowls and glasses on the table.

"You know Dad, Chad," Rick said. "Once something gets his attention, he'll be all over it."

"Amen to that," Frederick added. "He is like a bloodhound on the hunt!"

Pepper couldn't help saying, "I'd say the three of you have contributed to the development of his keen sense that something suspect might be happening with the escapades you've been involved in over the years."

Everyone started laughing. Even the triplets joined in, acknowledging that they were aware of their mischievous behavior growing up.

For sure, their parents often had their hands full!

I felt sure their wavy blond hair and sea-green eyes, along with their dimpled smiles, helped get them out of some of their naughtiness.

"What do you think will happen next?" Miguel asked.

"I could tell by the way my dad examined the two bills that he suspected that they weren't legit. If nothing else, the rank odor would signal something wasn't right. I felt sorry for Smudges when she put one in her mouth."

We all grimaced.

Chad went on to speculate that tomorrow his dad would check records for documentation about the information we had shared with him. If the facts didn't add up – and Chad knew they wouldn't – his dad would be on a mission to get to the bottom of things. Chad felt sure his dad would secretly begin an internal investigation.

"I say," my brother suggested, "now that a seed of mistrust has been planted, let's go enjoy the rest of the afternoon and go bowling."

Everyone agreed.

****

When Chad arrived at the police station on Monday afternoon, everything was moving along normally. He immediately went to his desk and began completing the items that Officer Rodriquez had left for him to do.

Throughout the afternoon, Chad kept wondering if maybe the gang's plan had hit a hitch. Little did he know that his dad had indeed discovered that there was no documentation of money being turned in or claimed.

Instead of confronting Officer Rodriquez, Chief Hankins immediately met with trusted officers who had worked in the department for years. He instructed some of them to patrol and check out areas with abandoned buildings. Others were assigned to remain in the office to keep an eye on Officer Rodriquez, along with making phone calls to the places where the officer had worked in his career. Looking for a connection, his dad specifically wanted to know if counterfeiting had been prevalent in the places the officer had been employed. He, his lead detective, and a couple of other officers would be checking out the area near the dog park. His dad had recognized the odor from the hundred-dollar-bills. Certain chemicals had been used for machinery manufacturing in those old buildings near the dog park. Chief Hankins was hoping for a break in the counterfeiting operation that had been widespread in Pandora for the past few months.

****

Chad had finished up his assigned duties. He was feeling restless that nothing seemed to be going as he and the gang had hoped. Thirty more minutes and he would be out of there. His brothers and friends were going to be disappointed that he wouldn't have any news to share.

As Chad was clearing off his desk for his return on Wednesday afternoon, Chief Hankins came into the department, followed by three others. All four men had serious expressions of their faces as they entered his dad's office.

Chad nearly jumped out of his chair when a few minutes later, his dad came to the entrance of his office and ordered both he and his mentor to come into the room.

Not suspecting anything to be wrong, Officer Rodriquez quickly rose from his chair with a smile as he entered the office. Chad purposely put a blank expression on his face. Looking his dad in the eye told him immediately that fat was about to hit the fire. He and his brothers had encountered that threatening look several times over the years. Chad was praying that this time it wouldn't be directed toward him.

No sooner had his dad shut the door that the seriousness of the situation dawned on his mentor. A frightened expression appeared on his face as he saw a stack of hundred-dollar bills on Chief Hankins's desk. His first instinct was to run. Anticipating his reaction, the other three men in the room were blocking the exit.

Over the next few minutes Chad's dad began to detail the events of the day. The counterfeiting operation in town had been discovered in one of the buildings across from the dog park. Five people were arrested at the scene. Officer Rodriquez's wife and two other couples were being processed this very minute in the back of the station. Checking with other police forces that Officer Rodriquez had previously worked at validated his participation as a counterfeiter. His record of employment with those police departments coincided with counterfeiting in those communities.

During the explanation, he would look at Chad from time to time, watching for a reaction. Knowing how his father operated when he was interrogating the triplets, it was important that Chad's reaction to the news was shocked. It was imperative that he act totally clueless about the info being shared.

Before reading Officer Rodriquez his rights, Chief Hankins turned to Chad and said, "The Barkleys' dog is a hero! Her uncovering of the two hundred-dollar-bills while you and Heather were on a walk yesterday gave us the break we needed to solve the counterfeit operation in Pandora. As soon as I smelled the stench from the money, I recognized the odor.

There were times when patrolling the area of the two machinery manufacturing plants, that awful smell permeated the air around the facilities."

If looks could kill, Chad knew he would be nine feet under. His now ex-mentor shot him an evil glare.

Ignoring his look, Chad said, "I can't wait to share with Heather that her little sister's dog helped solve a case in Pandora!"

17

Celebrations Galore

Since it was a Monday night, Chad was swamped with homework. The gang of seven would be eating lunch together at school tomorrow. His text was short for obvious reasons. It was important that no news be shared in writing.

Being such a gorgeous day with the sun shining brightly from a blue cloudless sky and a slight breeze, the seven of us were eating outside at a picnic table. I could tell that none of our minds were much on food. We wanted to know the status of the counterfeit operation.

As Chad outlined everything that had gone down yesterday, we all sat in complete silence. I'm sure the look on all our faces could only be described as amazement. The plan that we had put into motion turned out better than anyone of us could have predicted.

During Chad's depiction of the events, he clarified why the fake bills we had come across smelled awful. Officer Rodriquez and the other five turned on each other after their arrests. They were yelling insults at each other. One of the other couples had insisted that the last batch of bills they had made should have been destroyed. One of them had accidently dropped the pile in some old chemicals that were under the table they were using for their operation. However, the others disagreed that it was no big deal. They felt the air would eventually help the smell evaporate. Of course, that decision would be their downfall. For months, their illegal setup had gone well. Whether it was greed, laziness, or just plain stupidity on their part, keeping the rank bills had led to them being caught.

When Chad finished speaking, Pepper said, "I have a gut feeling that even without the potent odor, they would eventually have been caught. Remember, we knew that Officer Rodriquez was dishonest when he told you about the old man's story and the ATM."

"True," Chad agreed. "It would have taken a little longer and probably a more complex plan would have needed to be implemented."

Everyone nodded in agreement.

"From this moment on we need to remember our pact," Miguel reminded everyone. "No more discussion among us."

"If someone brings the counterfeiting subject up, we should acknowledge the great job the Pandora Police Department did in solving the case," Rick added.

"We can't forget that your dad said Smudges was a hero!" I said.

"That's right, Sis! We can always direct the conversation to Lizzie's Portie."

For once, the gang of seven would not be in the spotlight! We gave each other high fives in celebration of a game plan well executed!

****

Homecoming festivities were off to a fantastic start! The Pandora Panthers had just won the homecoming game. The other team didn't even get on the scoreboard. We had seven touchdowns. Coach Chester – called Chesty by all the students when he wasn't around - strutted around with his chest puffed out whenever his team scored. Pepper, the Icky triplets, and I couldn't help looking at each other and giggling throughout the entire game. Later, everyone drove around town honking their horns in celebration of the defeat! Stopping for ice cream at Taborn's was included.

****

I had a hard time sleeping last night. My excitement for the Pandora Homecoming Dance was keeping me awake. I could hardly wait for morning to come. I kept visualizing myself with Chad by my side. He would be wearing a gold tie to match my dress. Miguel had also agreed to wear a tie to match Pepper's turquoise outfit, along with Rick doing the same to match Amelia's clothes. Jeff and Frederick were going stag. There would be plenty of girls to dance with throughout the evening.

****

The dance was in full swing. I knew I would be having dreams about this night for quite some time. My friends and I danced almost every dance. We laughed and laughed the entire evening. Secretly we were unbelievably happy that we were not in the spotlight or on our parents' radar. Life was good!

Epilogue

Police Chief Hankins declared, "The town of Pandora would like to celebrate a special dog that helped the Pandora Police Department to solve the counterfeit operation in our community. Smudges, a Portugal water dog, is our HERO! Her owner, Lizzie Barkley, will be accepting a medal in her honor."

The crowd went wild! The gang of seven clapped the loudest, along with having the widest grins of everyone.

A Note from the Author

Dear Reader,

I hope you have enjoyed reading my trilogy series, The Mysterious Icicle, The Mysterious Firefly, and The Mysterious Cache as much as I did in writing the stories!

Hope you will check out other books that I have written and others to come.

~Candy Moore Myers

Miracles All Around Us
Dudley's Miraculous Christmas
Friends Forever
The Perfect You
Angels From Above
Character Building ABCs
Jungle Critters to the Rescue
Bindy Bear's Hooray Day
Toby's Search for the Perfect Pet

www.ingramcontent.com/pod-product-compliance
Ingram Content Group UK Ltd.
Pitfield, Milton Keynes, MK11 3LW, UK
UKHW050459161224
452383UK00014BA/101/J

9 798330 618965